In Memory of
Mary Margaret Cox
1919 - 2010

# Frankie Stein

by

Lola M. Schaefer

illustrated by

Kevan Atteberry

Marshall Cavendish Children

Marshall Cavendish Corporation, 99 White Plains Road, Tarrytown, NY 10591
www.marshallcavendish.us/kids

Library of Congress Cataloging-in-Publication Data
Schaefer, Lola M., 1950–
Frankie Stein / by Lola M. Schaefer ; illustrated by Kevan J. Atteberry. — 1st ed.
p. cm.
Summary: Mr. and Mrs. Frank N. Stein love their son very much, but despite their best efforts and his, it seems he will never
look or act as scary as a Stein should.
ISBN: 978-0-7614-5358-1 (hardcover) ISBN: 978-0-7614-5608-7 (paperback)
[1. Individuality—Fiction. 2. Monsters—Fiction. 3. Family life—Fiction.]  I. Atteberry, Kevan, ill. II. Title.
PZ7.S33233Fra 2007
[E]—dc22
2007000256


The illustrations are rendered in Adobe Illustrator and Photoshop.
Book design by Anahid Hamparian
Editor: Margery Cuyler


Printed in Malaysia
First Marshall Cavendish paperback edition, 2009
3  5  6  4  2

**mc Marshall Cavendish**
Children

For Wyatt

—L.M.S.


For my two monsters, Lennon and Rio

—K.A.

**Frankie Stein** came into the world on a bright, sunny day.

"Our son!" announced his proud parents, and they rushed to his side.

"Oh my," said his mother. "He's . . . cute."

"Why doesn't he look scary like us?" asked his father.

"I don't know," said his mother. "But with our help, I'm sure he will."

Mr. and Mrs. Frank N. Stein showered their son with scariness.

They made faces at him.

They shouted **BOO!** and **GOTCHA!**

And every night they read him stories by candlelight.

One day, while feeding Frankie, his father
was shocked to see a lock of sun-gold hair.

"What's this?" he asked.

"I can take care of that,"
said his mother.

When Frankie got his first tooth,
it was white.

"What's this?" asked his mother.

"I can take care of that," said
his father.

During a game of peek-a-boo, Frankie's face shone pink and smooth.

"We can take care of that," said his parents.

Little by little, Frankie began to look like a Stein.

FACE SPOTS

BUMP STICKERS

"I'm starting to see a resemblance,"
said his mother.

"Yes, but he still isn't all that scary," said his father.

"That's true," said his mother. "But at least Frankie can act scary like us!"

"Indeed!" said his father.

Mrs. Frank N. Stein taught Frankie how to walk.

"Hold your arms out straight," said his mother.

Frankie did.

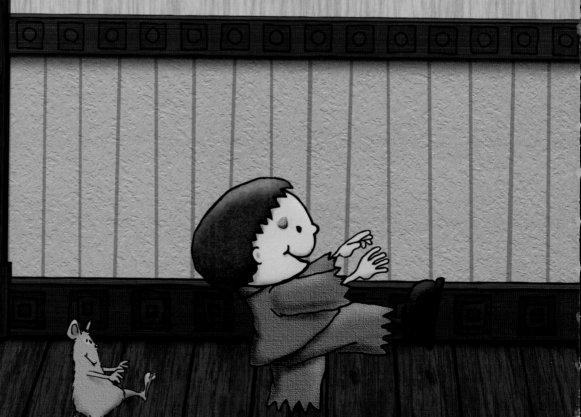

"Now take big, slow steps," she said. "Like this."

Frankie tried. He really did. But his walk was more of a bounce.

Mr. Frank N. Stein taught
Frankie how to moan.

"Open your mouth wide,"
said his father.

Frankie did.

"Now, groan long and loud,"
he said. "Like this.

# ohhhhhhhh!"

Frankie tried. He really did. But his
moan was more of a squeak.
"oooh! oooh!"

"Well, Frankie might not have all our scary looks," said his mother.

"And he might not act scary like us," said his father.

"But he is a Stein," they said.
"Maybe he just needs a little inspiration."

That night, Frankie's
mother and father pulled
the family tree from
the closet.

"This is your uncle
Franklin," said Mr. Frank
N. Stein to his son.
"His laugh turns men to stone."

Frankie chuckled.

"Here is your great-granddaddy Frank
the Gripper," said Mrs. Frank N. Stein.
"He can hold the attention of an entire town."

Francois

Aunt Fran

Uncle Franklin

Grannie Frances

"And this is your grandmother Frances,"
said Mr. and Mrs. Frank N. Stein.

"She's always full of surprises," said

Aunt Francesca

Cousin Francisco

Uncle Fr...

Uncl...

Fr...

Frank the Gripper

"So, you see, son," said Frankie's father, "you come from a long line of Steins, each one different but scary."

"Indeed," said Frankie, studying each family member, "and I'll be scary, too. Just wait and see."

For the next few weeks, Frankie stayed in his room and practiced

# SCARY. ✦

Frankie tried and tried, but he just couldn't look or act like his parents.

Instead, Frankie decided on his own kind of scary.

Early one morning,
Frankie made a grand
appearance.

"Well, what do you think?" he asked his parents.

"Horrifying!" yelled his mother and father.
They threw their hands in front of their faces.

"If you think that's scary," said Frankie, "watch this."
He wrapped his arms around his parents and hugged
them tight.

"Spine-tingling!" blurted Mr. and Mrs. Frank N. Stein
between gasps.

Then Frankie leaned close and gave them each a big,
lip-smacking kiss.

Mr. and Mrs. Frank N. Stein clutched their hearts.

# "SCARY!"

they shrieked, and they fainted dead away.

From that day forward,
Frankie Stein was considered
the scariest Stein of all . . .

until Francie Stein came into the world.